and the

Big Quiz

Barbara Catchpole

Illustrated by Dynamo

Ransom

Th-wump!

Th-wump! My Maths book flew through the air, flapping its pages like a mad bird. Then it hit the kitchen wall.

It just missed Raj and landed on Harry, who was out for a walk around the kitchen. Harry kept on going, with the book on his back. He looked like a little furry tortoise - then he dashed under the cupboard to hide.

I wailed:

    'I can't do this bloomin' homework! The

teachers didn't explain it properly. I don't get it! I hate Maths!'

I wail a lot in Maths.

Dogs hate homework

Homework is nuts! Do you get homework at your school? Bonkers, right?

You work all day at school, learning about stuff like the Amazon rainforest and the offside rule, and then they give you more random stuff to do at

home. Stuff like 'Pretend you are a Roman', or
Page 49 'Make up a recipe with pineapples in it'.

You don't want to do it and they don't want to
mark it. So why
bother? And it's hard
to imagine you're a
Roman while you're
watching Eastenders.

So much can go wrong with homework, anyway!
We all have a homework diary so we don't
forget what our homework is. I kept forgetting
where I put my diary. So Mum bought me a
notebook so I could write in it where I put my
homework diary.

Guess what? Yes, I forgot where I left the notebook. No, I'm not getting another book to remind me where the book is that reminds me where my homework book is. I'd end up with a lorry-load of books following me everywhere.

Then I'd need a book to write down where I'd parked the lorry.

I write it all on my arms now. But that doesn't

work very well if you have to have a bath.
That's another really good reason to say dirty.

We get far too much homework as well. Those
books are heavy! The little kids get so much
homework that their backpacks weigh a ton. You
only have to push them backwards and they fall
on their backs, so their
little legs wiggle in the air.
Like little upside-down
flies wearing backpacks.

They can't get up again on their own (the little
kids I mean, not the flies. But flies wearing
backpacks probably can't get up, either.) They
have to wait for their mums to come and help.

Then you forget the books you need. You take home 'Maths for You' instead of 'Maths for Everyone', or you take home the wrong writing book (all mine are red, except for the one Vampire Baby was sick on – the colour came out a bit on that one).

Then your drink bottle leaks all over your books, or you end up trying to do ten homeworks on the same night. So you tell your teacher the dog ate it. I think I should buy a dog.

Ten best homework excuses from our class

1. 'I put it in the freezer with the shopping and didn't find it until a week too late. The Cornettos were stuck to it.'

2. 'My school bag was stolen by an albatross.'

3. 'My religion won't let me work on Tuesdays, Wednesdays or Thursdays.'

4. 'I had to go to the doctor's / dentist's / foot guy / child psychologist.' Zac said that. Zac has been going to the child psychologist since he was three and ate his mum's

lipstick. It's not doing anybody any good.

5. 'My mouse ate it, then
    my snake ate my mouse.'

6. 'My mum tied me up.'

7. 'It caught fire, right in front of my eyes.
    My dad said things do that sometimes.'

8. 'I got so excited pretending I was a
    Roman, I went out of the house wearing a
    toga. I got locked out in my bedsheet and
    the lady next door called the police. She's
    never liked us because of the big tree in
    our back garden.'

9. 'I dropped it down the toilet on the plane to Malaga.'

10. 'My dog ate my locker key and we had to go to the vets. We're still waiting for it to have a poo.'

Tonight's homework

Mum yelled:

    'Pick that book up, Pig!'

    'No! You threw it, Mum!'

Why did Mum throw my Maths book at the wall? I was drawing Pokemon characters in the margin and getting round to doing my Maths homework. You have to think a lot in Maths, and drawing Pokemons (Pokemen?) helps me think.

Mum decided to 'help me get started'. She had just done the first sum:

$$2b(3c - 2a)$$

and she got the answer:

a banana.

Then she threw the book and shouted a bit. If Raj had looked up, it would have hit him.

14

After a while, Harry came out from under the cupboard where he was hiding, and started to nibble a corner of the book. Wicked! That was my excuse – my hamster ate my homework!

Raj is not a kind boy

That was when Raj told Mum about the Big Quiz. Raj spends more time in our house than I do. I think Mum likes him better than me too, but Mrs Kaur won't swap. I think Mum asked and Mrs Kaur said 'no'.

Raj had been chucked out of his house for underlining his answers too noisily. He likes to underline his answers twice in red ink with a ruler, and one of his brain-box sisters was studying to be Prime Minister or something and needed ABSOLUTE SILENCE. (That's much quieter than absolute silence.)

Raj was making too much noise picking up his ruler and breathing. So he was round ours again.

Raj said:

    'Never mind, Mrs Green, just you sit down on the sofa and I'll make you a nice cup of tea.'

'Thank you, Rajesh, you are a kind boy.'

No he wasn't! He was trying to get me to join his Quiz Team. I know his sneaky little ways! Grown-ups give into him because he sucks up to them:

'Yes, Mrs Green. No, Mrs Green. You look lovely today, Mrs Green.'

Mum says I should try it, but nobody would believe me. I would say:

'You look lovely today, Mum,'

and she would say:

'What are you after Pig? Are you in trouble again at school? Is it stink bombs or that bloomin' plastic poo?'

Nobody wanted to be in the quiz

There were loads of reasons why no one wanted to be in the quiz except Raj and Min Lee (girl with big fringe and glasses, in case you're wondering. The girl has the glasses, not the fringe. Got to be clear.).

Spurs were playing Arsenal that night and most of the dads didn't want to go to the quiz.

Nobody wanted to go without their dads seeing them. I didn't either, although my dad was in Spain, not in front of Sky Sports.

The quiz was against The Academy, with their glass school and their perfect uniforms. Even their teeth are whiter than ours. They smell nice and they know things. They've got blazers instead of sweatshirts, and a big sports hall.

Raj and Min aren't cool. Raj is my mate and he's been my friend since Reception, but he is a bit of a boff. He'd asked loads of people to be in this quiz thing and nobody had said 'yes'.

In fact, loads of people were a bit rude. Dean said he was moving house to Iceland and Saffron said she was going to the dentist and her mouth would be wired up.

Tiffany said she would rather chew her own

arm off. Saffron said she would like to chew her own arm off, but her mouth would be wired up. Zac had to go to the child psychologist – his mum was missing loads of lipstick.

Thing is, Raj is clever and good at getting his own way. And there he was, talking to my mum about the quiz! I had to stop him!

I leapt onto the sofa and slapped my hands over Raj's mouth, but it was too late.

Mum said:

> 'You are going on that quiz, Pig! It's going to be on TV! Television! The whole country will see my good-looking, clever little boy.'

Raj smiled. It was a cunning smile.

Angry

I was livid! I pushed Raj out into the back
yard, by Mum's pile of rocks and Suki's pile of
fag ends, and shouted at him.

A cat stopped doing its business and ran away.

Mrs Zielinski's dog started shouting:

'Ralph! Ralph!'

I shouted:

'You complete divvy! I don't want to be in your stupid quiz! We are going to lose 149 – nil, you complete and utter wazzock!'

Raj laughed.

'Thanks, Pig! I knew you'd do it!'

He'd planned this. He'd even written lists of things we had to learn. Before asking us! Mine was capital cities and flags.

I tried to be a bit clearer:

'No! No way! No! Get it? No! No. No. No. No!!'

Raj went quiet then and looked at the floor a bit. He kicked a rock.

'I really want to win this quiz, Pig. All my sisters are doing exams and getting mad jobs and Mum tells all the aunties about it on the phone. I want to do something too! I want to win! I want to hear Mum banging on about it!'

'Then why are you asking me to do it? I

don't know anything!' (Good point, I thought!)

Raj kicked another rock quite hard and blinked a lot. He wasn't crying – the cold air got in his eyes. Suddenly I knew what was going on. Nobody else would do it for him – I was the last choice. It was just like picking teams in football lessons.

Raj looked really sad. I wouldn't like to have seven sisters. I didn't even want the one I had got. (Imagine having seven Sukis! That would be like putting your head in a blender every hour, forever. It would be against human rights or something.)

'Oh alright – I'll have a go.'
After all, he was my best mate.

Flags

Now here's the thing – there's loads of neat stuff in countries.

There's parrots and penguins and mountains and waterfalls and volcanoes. There's pasta and cream cakes and chips. There's surfing and space rockets and ski runs.

So what do countries put on their flags? Stripes, more stripes, moons and stars! That's more or less it. Flag-designers have got no imagination! It's not like it's a hard job.

It's impossible to remember which boring flag belongs to which boring country.

Take Ireland and the Côte d'Ivoire (you say 'coat Dee vuwah') wherever that is. Both countries have the same flags – a bunch of stripes, same size, same colours – just in a different order. That's it! In real life Ireland has leprechauns

27

and shamrocks and stuff and the Côte d'Ivoire

has ... has ... well – I bet it has loads of cool

stuff.

Yep, googled it! Côte d'Ivoire has elephants and

cocoa beans and cool footballers.

And they chose an orange stripe! Why? Why?

Why?

I bet the flag-designer person couldn't draw elephants or leprechauns. Or anything else except straight lines.

Anyway, Mum tested me on flags and capitals. I got three right out of thirty. When I told her Rome was in Latvia we both went 'Ooooff!' and we had to have a rest and eat some chips.

Mum said:

> 'Never mind, perhaps there'll be a power cut.'

What my family knows

Most of the rounds of the quiz were going to be 'buzz in' ones, where you press a buzzer if you think you know the right answer.

Those rounds would be fine. I'd just keep my hands in my pockets and tuck my elbows in so I couldn't do any damage.

But there was one round where you got questions to yourself. They did this so that you could look a

complete divvy on
television when you
got them wrong.
Why else would
they do it?

I was all stressy about that round. I wanted
to help Raj, but I didn't want all Britain (and
the rest of the world watching it on the
internet) knowing I was an idiot.

I told Mum about it. She phoned Bob for advice.
Then she told me the best thing to do was to
ask each member of my family for a bit of
their knowledge. Perhaps I would get lucky!

Mum:

'Bees have five eyes.'

'Ay?'

I couldn't believe I'd heard her right.

'And butterflies taste with their feet.

Remember that, Pig! It's important! And

say 'pardon' not 'ay'. '

Gran:

'Yorkshire puddings go all flat if you keep opening the oven.'

Suki:

'Waterproof mascara is impossible to get off. I also know what's going to happen to you if you keep asking me bloomin' stupid questions. Want me to show you? Do you? Do you?'

Santa told me what horse was going to win the 3:30 race. (It lost.) (In fact it came last.) (It nearly won the 4:00, it was so slow.)

(Anyway, no quiz person was going to ask me 'Who is going to win ... last week's 3.30?')

I was doomed.

You're going down, Speccy!

'It's Speccyman and Carrot Head – two superheroes – not!'

That was what the leader of the other team said to us! I just wanted to punch him – a really hard punch. What an idiot!

Bob had driven me to the quiz (it was held at the Academy, of course). I had to sit in the back of the car, with the ugly pots and the cats.

Bob said he wanted to have a chat with the guy who did the quiz. They had been to art college together or something. While they were nattering on, the leader of the Academy Team came over to Raj.

The boy was wearing the Academy Blazer with its motto: 'To the skies!' He was wearing a name badge which said 'Dom'.

Raj was wearing our horrible purple sweatshirt with its motto: 'Dig deeper!' And his name badge said 'Rajesh'.

Dom was very tall. Raj was very short.

Dom was very loud. Raj was very quiet.

Dom was very good-looking. Raj was Raj.

And Dom said it:

> 'It's Speccyman and Carrot Head – two
> superheroes – not!'

He got right close to Raj and he was spitting a
bit. I hate it when people do that! It's not
right. If you know you spit, don't say anything!

His face was angry.

> 'What do you know? Not much I bet! We

are going to win by hundreds of points! By thousands! By gazillions! Then you can all crawl back to your smelly little school! Got it, Four-eyes? Goggle-face? You lot are going down! You're going down, Speccy!'

Then he said, smiling all of a sudden, as the quiz bloke came to get us:

'And jolly good luck! May the best team win!'

Raj wiped his face and looked at me. Suddenly I really, really wanted to win.

Bob's boy

The Quiz Bloke was really nice. He said:

'So you're Bob's boy?'

'Yeah.'

I didn't know what to say really. Bob's not my dad and he nags me a lot and he's boring, but in a way ...

'Yeah, he's my ... Bob.'

The Quiz

I bet you're thinking:

'At last! I'm reading this book because he said it was about a quiz, and it's taken him bloomin' ages to get round to it.'

You could have read the end bit of the book first. I do that. Sometimes I don't even bother reading the first bit.

The actual quiz went by really quickly. I could hear my family shouting out. They were the noisiest family there by miles.

Because it was night time, Vampire Baby started screaming and Mum was asked to take him out. I could hear her arguing and then having a bit  of a shout at some bloke from the Academy:

'Get your hands off me! I'm not going nowhere!'

Whenever we got one right Suki shouted:

'Go bro!'

Santa roared:

'Get in there!'

Gran was waving her walking stick and blowing a vuvuzela – until the Academy bloke took it off her.

Raj and Min were amazing. They kept buzzing and answering:

'18th century.'

'White blood cells.'

'The Mad Hatter.'

'False!'

'True!'

'Pineapple upside down cake!'

'Off-side!'

There was nothing they didn't know. Raj had

told me not to answer, even if I was really

sure I knew the answer, so I said nothing.

I didn't know anything anyway.

The solo round

Then came the round
where I had to answer.
My tummy went all
bubbly.

These were my questions:

'How many eyes does a bee have?'

'Five!'

'Cor-rect!'

And:

'How does a butterfly taste things?'

'With its feet.'

'Cor-rect!'

How lucky was that?
I looked like a raving
genius!

It was a tie

It was really close. There were just three
questions left and the score was 20 – 20. The
hall went quiet (except for Vampire Baby, who
was shouting 'Oh-oh, oh-oh, oh-oh').

'What did Romans wear? Rajesh – Coalpits High School!'

'A toga.'

'Cor-rect!'

21–20 to us.

I was dying for a wee and I was really hungry. Also my head itched at the back and I didn't want to scratch it in case everyone thought I had nits. The more I tried not to think about it, the more it itched. Perhaps I did have nits!

Then I could actually feel them. They were

crawling all over my
head, holding a little
party, drinking Nit Cola
and eating Nit Jelly.
They started a Nit
Conga. I bet they were
waving at the camera.

'Next question: where do the trees form a
canopy? Lee King, the Academy.'

Lee King! He was called Lee King – like leaking.
What were his parents thinking? The word
'leaking' made me want a wee even more.

'The Amazon rainforest.'

'Cor-rect!'

Both schools on 21 points. It was all on the last question.

> 'OK – think carefully before you answer –
> this is a multiple-choice question. Here it is.
> Three point one four.
> Is it a) pi   b) tart or   c) pizza?'

Now what happened was, I put my hand up because I really had to scratch a bit. As it came down, it hit the buzzer by mistake.

'Peter Ian Green, Coalpits High School.'

I didn't understand the question at all, but I had to answer. What could I do? Perhaps if I heard it again? So I said:

'Ay?'

'Cor-rect!'

The silence stretched on ...

Then suddenly someone was shouting:

'Yes! Yes! We've won! Go, Pits!'

It was our head teacher, Miss Joseph. She was jumping up and down in the audience like a lunatic. Then she got into the middle bit and did a little dance, waggling her bottom and singing:

'We beat you, we beat you!'

The whole audience started shouting and I could see my family rushing to the stage.

Min hugged me and Raj went to hug me and

then wasn't sure, and then hugged me anyway.
He had a huge grin on his face and his mum
was shouting:

'That's my Rajesh! He is a genius!'

Mum climbed up on the
stage and planted a great
big kiss on my face, right
in front of the camera,
which was horrible. I
was a hero!

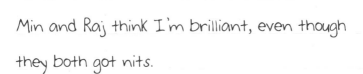

Min and Raj think I'm brilliant, even though
they both got nits.

It was a good job I didn't say 'Pardon'.

The next **PIG** book is

PIG
gets
Angry

About the author

Barbara Catchpole was a teacher for thirty years and enjoyed every minute. She has three sons of her own who were always perfectly behaved and never gave her a second of worry.

Barbara also tells lies.